Caught Red-handed!

Frank tried to pull away from Zack. As he slipped back, Frank's backpack slid down his arm. As Frank went to pull it back up, Zack grabbed it in his hand. The two boys began to tug back and forth on Frank's bookbag.

"Let go!" Frank yelled.

Just then the backpack's zipper broke. A large book with a green cover fell to the ground.

"Well, what do we have here?" Zack said. *"Novick's Big Book of Baseball Statistics.* What a surprise!"

Frank just stared at the book on the ground.

"Frank Hardy is the book thief!" Zack shouted.

Frank and Joe Hardy: The Clues Brothers

Available from MINSTREL BOOKS

WHO TOOK THE BOOK?

Franklin W. Dixon

Illustrated by
Marcy Ramsey

A
MINSTREL®
BOOK

Published by POCKET BOOKS
New York   London   Toronto   Sydney   Tokyo   Singapore

A MINSTREL PAPERBACK *Original*

 A Minstrel Book published by
POCKET BOOKS, a division of Simon & Schuster Inc.
1230 Avenue of the Americas, New York, NY 10020

Copyright © 1998 by Simon & Schuster Inc.

Produced by Mega-Books, Inc.

ISBN: 0-671-00407-7

First Minstrel Books printing May 1998

10 9 8 7 6 5 4 3 2 1

Cover art by Thompson Studio

Printed in the U.S.A.

1

Trouble Before School

Frank, your zipper is down."

Eight-year-old Joe Hardy and his nine-year-old brother, Frank, were walking to school. It was a Monday morning.

"What?" Frank said. He stopped walking.

"The zipper on your backpack," Joe said. "It's open."

Frank pushed a few pieces of paper into his backpack. Then he zipped it all the way closed.

"Thank you," he said. "I don't want to lose my math homework."

Frank and Joe came to the end of their block. Then they turned the corner.

"They're right on time," Frank said. He looked up the street. Chet Morton and his younger sister, Iola, were walking toward them.

Chet was in the same fourth-grade class as Frank. He had been the first friend Frank and Joe had made when they moved to Bayport. Iola was Chet's seven-year-old sister.

"Hi!" Joe called out.

Chet was carrying four books, some pieces of paper, and a banana. He was trying to peel the banana, hold the books, and walk at the same time.

"Be careful," Frank told Chet.

But it was too late. Chet's books slid out of his hands. When they hit the ground, papers scattered in every direction.

"You banana-head!" Iola giggled.

Then she bent down to help her brother pick up what he had dropped.

Frank and Joe helped, too. Frank took some books from the ground.

"Where's your backpack?" Frank asked Chet.

"It's being washed," Iola answered for her brother. "Chet forgot to tighten the lid on his lunch last week. It spilled all over the inside of the backpack."

"Pea soup," Chet said. "What a mess."

"Well, I couldn't live without my backpack," Frank said. "I carry everything I need for school in here."

The four friends began to walk toward school.

"Guess what I did on Saturday," Iola said.

"I give up," Frank said. "What did you do on Saturday?"

"I went to a slumber party at Tanya Wilkins's house," Iola answered.

"Can you believe it?" Chet asked.

"Tanya had a party with second graders there!"

Tanya was in fourth grade. She was also on the school basketball team with Frank.

"She invited girls from all different classes," Iola said. She looked at Joe. "She had some girls from Joe's class there," she added.

"So?" Joe asked. "Why should I care?"

"Someone there was talking about you," Iola said. She smiled a big smile at Joe.

"Who talked about me?" Joe asked.

"My lips are sealed," Iola said. She pretended to close a big zipper across her mouth.

The group arrived at the school. Mike Mendez and Tony Prito, two boys from Joe's class, were already there.

"Hey, everyone!" Mike called as he trotted over.

Just then Tanya Wilkins and Wendy

4

Kay joined the group. Wendy was in Joe's class. She lived two houses down from Tanya, and the two girls were friends.

"Hey, everybody," Tanya said.

"Good morning, *Joey*," Wendy said. She pushed her way into the group and stood close to Joe.

"Hi, Wen . . . Wend . . . ah-choo!" Joe sneezed. He sneezed again. Then he coughed.

"Oh, Joe," Wendy said. "You must have a cold."

"I don't have a cold." Joe coughed again. "At least, I don't think I have a cold."

Joe turned and talked to Tony. "Did you do the history homework?" Joe asked.

"Of course," Tony answered. "My dad said I had to finish it before I could watch the basketball game on TV."

"All you ever think about is basketball," Joe said. "Baseball is better."

"I agree," Mike said. "Baseball is the best."

"Baseball is boring," Tony said. "There's never more than a couple of minutes of action in baseball."

"No way!" Joe replied. "Each pitch has action."

"Joe's right," Wendy said. "Baseball is much better than basketball."

"Did you come to the basketball game on Saturday?" Tanya asked. "Now, that had action."

"Better believe I did!" Tony said. Tony pretended he was dribbling a basketball. "Eight seconds left," he said.

Frank dropped his backpack and ran a few feet to the left. Then he circled around Joe.

"Hardy breaks for the basket," Joe said. "And it's *in!* Two points for Hardy." Joe was pretending to be a sportscaster.

"Prito passes to Mendez," Tony said. He threw the pretend basketball to Mike.

Mike caught it. He pretended to dribble to his right.

"Mendez behind the back to Wilkins." Mike flipped the pretend ball to Tanya.

"Wilkins launches it toward the basket," Tanya shouted.

Frank jumped high up into the air. "And Hardy slams it—ooph!" Frank crashed down to the ground, right into Zack Jackson.

Zack and his best friend, Peter "Dribbles" Libretti, had just walked onto the playground. Zack fell backward into Dribbles. All three boys tumbled to the ground.

"That's it, Hardy," Zack said. He stood up and brushed himself off. Then he looked down at Frank.

"It's all over for you, Hardy."

2

A Close Call

It was an accident," Frank said.

"Yeah, he didn't mean it," Joe said. He ran to stand next to his brother.

Dribbles got up from the ground and stood next to Zack. Zack folded his arms across his chest.

"Accident? You and your brother here sure have a lot of accidents with us two as targets," Zack said. "You poured popcorn over my head at the movies. Then you got Dribbles in trouble at basketball tryouts."

"Yeah," Dribbles said. "I think you two are trying to pick a fight with us."

"Us?" Joe was surprised by what Dribbles was saying. "You two are the ones who are always getting in our way."

"Are you threatening us?" Dribbles asked. He grinned at Zack. "I think they just challenged us."

"We didn't—" Frank started to say.

"I like a challenge," Zack said. "But pounding these two babies will have to do instead."

Zack pushed Frank. Frank took a few steps backward. He almost fell.

The other kids on the playground ran over to see what was going on.

Just then a loud bell rang. It was time to go inside and start school.

Everyone who had been standing outside began to walk to the school entrance. No one wanted to get into trouble by being late to class.

"You're off the hook this time, Hardy," Zack said loudly. "Let's go, Dribbles."

Zack and Dribbles turned and walked away. Frank and Joe were the only two left on the playground.

"That was a close call. Are you okay?" Joe asked his brother.

"I'm fine," Frank answered. "Let's go inside."

"One day the Zack Pack and the Hardy brothers are going to have it out once and for all," Joe said.

"Maybe, maybe not," Frank told his brother. "Getting angry might only make things worse."

Frank and Joe walked inside. Frank headed for Mrs. Burton's classroom. Joe walked to Mrs. Adair's third-grade class.

Both brothers thought about their showdown with Zack and Dribbles all morning.

Just before lunch Frank and Joe got a chance to talk again. This time they were in the library. Both of their teachers had assigned them research projects to do.

As Frank's class walked into the li-

11

brary, he saw Joe. "Do you feel less angry now?" Frank asked.

"A little," Joe said. He nodded his head toward the spot where Zack and Dribbles were sitting. "What kind of research are those two doing? I didn't think they could read."

"No talking, boys."

Joe and Frank looked up to see the smiling face of Ms. Goldberg, the school librarian. She had wavy, bright red hair.

"Sorry, Ms. Goldberg," Frank said.

"That's all right, boys," Ms. Goldberg said. "And what sort of research are you doing?" she asked.

"We're studying about gravity in Mrs. Adair's class," Joe said. "You know— why things fall. My report is about what makes a curve ball curve."

"Baseball, baseball, baseball," Frank said to Ms. Goldberg. "That's all he ever talks about."

"Very interesting topic, Joe," Ms. Goldberg said. She turned to Frank. "And what are you working on?"

"We're studying statistics in Mrs. Burton's class."

"Really?" Ms. Goldberg said. "That sounds very advanced."

"It's not that complicated," Frank said. "Statistics are just about numbers," Frank said. "Like how many kids under nine have to do reports compared to how many kids over nine have to do reports. But I haven't figured out what kind of numbers I want to write about."

"I think I might have something over here that will interest both of you," Ms. Goldberg said.

The librarian turned and walked to the reference counter. Frank and Joe followed her. As the two brothers passed the table where Zack and Dribbles were sitting, they heard the bullies whisper, "Teacher's pet."

When Frank and Joe got to the counter, Joe noticed Wendy Kay stand-

ing at the counter. She was flipping through a large dictionary that was on a special stand next to the reference desk. Joe sneezed.

Ms. Goldberg walked behind the counter. Frank and Joe leaned against the front of the counter. Ms. Goldberg reached up to a high shelf. She turned around with a large book in her hands. It had a green cover with gold letters across the front. She put the book down carefully on the counter.

"Here it is, boys," she said. She turned the large book around so that Frank and Joe could read the title.

"*Novick's Big Book of Baseball Statistics*," Joe read. "Awesome!"

"I thought you'd like it," Ms. Goldberg said with a smile.

"I sure do," Joe said. He reached out and opened the book. "So, which one of us gets to check out the book?" Joe asked.

"I'm afraid neither one of you can actually take out the book," Ms. Goldberg said. "The book is very rare. It was lent to us by the Novick Private Library. It will be here for only one more day."

"I wish it could be here for more than a day," Frank said.

"I thought it might give you two some ideas for your projects," Ms. Goldberg said.

Just then Zack walked up to the reference desk. "What are you two clowns looking at?" he asked.

"A really cool book on baseball," Joe replied.

"Like I care," Zack said.

Joe and Frank both glared at Zack. Then they went back to looking at the book.

"Thanks for letting us see it," Frank said to Ms. Goldberg.

"We'd better get back to our reports," Joe said. "They're due at the end of the week."

Frank and Joe walked back to the table where they had left their work.

Suddenly the whole room went dark.

"What's going on?" Joe said.

"I think there's a power failure," Frank said. He reached into his backpack in the darkness. "Good thing I have my miniflashlight with me."

Frank began to walk toward the front of the library. He led the way in front of him with the tiny flashlight. Joe followed his brother.

A loud noise came from behind the two brothers. Frank turned around quickly and pointed the flashlight behind him. He and Joe saw a large shadow against the back wall of the library. They couldn't see who was behind them.

Just then the shadow disappeared and the lights came back on.

"Let's ask Ms. Goldberg what happened," Frank said. Frank and Joe walked to the reference desk.

"Somebody leaned against the light switch beside the library door," Ms. Goldberg said. "It happens all the time. It was just a natural mistake."

At lunch Frank and Joe told Chet, Mike, and Tony about the special book they had looked at. "I think I'm going to do my report on baseball statistics," Frank told the others.

After lunch Frank's class got a spelling test. Joe's class was learning about the tides of the ocean. Suddenly, Ms. Vaughn's voice came over the public address system.

"Attention, everyone," the principal said over the speaker in each classroom. "Ms. Goldberg has just told me that one of the books on loan to our library—*Novick's Big Book of Baseball Statistics*—is missing."

That's the book Frank and I looked at, Joe thought. And we were the last two people to look at it!

3

Who Took the Book?

Hey, Joe, is that the book you were telling me about?" Malcolm, the boy who sat in front of Joe, turned around in his seat.

Joe gulped. "Yes," he said, "but I didn't take it." He sank lower in his seat.

Ms. Vaughn's voice continued over the speaker. "I am hoping that the book was taken by accident. If it is returned to the library before the end of school today, no questions will be asked."

"I hope it's returned, Joe," Malcolm

said. "I wanted to get a look at it." Everyone in the classroom looked at Malcolm and Joe.

"Quiet down, everyone," Mrs. Adair said. "Does anybody here know anything about that book?"

"Joe does," Tony Prito said. "He was telling me about it during lunch."

Everyone in the class looked at Joe.

"Why is everybody looking at Joe?" Wendy Kay asked.

"Thanks a lot, Tony," Joe mumbled.

"Well, Joe?" Mrs. Adair said.

"I didn't take the book," Joe said. "I never even moved it from the counter. Ms. Goldberg told me and Frank that we couldn't check it out of the library."

Meanwhile, over in Mrs. Burton's class, Frank was the center of attention, too.

"I saw him and his brother looking at that book," Zack Jackson was saying loudly.

Everybody in the classroom looked at Frank.

"Yeah," Zack went on. "They were going on like little babies about how they wanted to take the book home."

"Hey, Joe and I would never steal anything," Frank said.

"Settle down, class!" Mrs. Burton said. "We are still in the middle of a spelling test, remember."

"Sorry, Mrs. Burton," Frank said.

"Sorry, Mrs. Burton," Zack said in exactly the same voice Frank had used.

Frank gave Zack an angry look. Zack made a face, pretending that he was scared.

Soon after Ms. Vaughn's announcement about the missing library book, school was over for the day. Joe hurried outside to meet Frank and Chet. The three friends discussed the library book while they walked home.

"That book was pretty valuable," Joe said. "I'd sure like to catch the thief."

"Yeah, especially since everybody thinks we took the book," Frank said.

"What makes you think the book was stolen?" Chet asked. "Ms. Vaughn just said it was missing."

"Good thinking, Chet," Frank said. "But you weren't in the library with me and Joe. Ms. Goldberg watched the book like a hawk."

"Yeah," Joe added. "She didn't let it out of her sight for a second."

"Well, then," Chet said, "this looks like another job for the Clues Brothers."

The Clues Brothers was the name that Mike Mendez had given Frank and Joe when they had solved their first case.

"We start first thing tomorrow morning," Frank said.

At dinner that night, Frank and Joe told their father about the missing library book. Mr. Hardy had been a police detective in New York City. Now that the Hardy family had moved to Bayport, he was a private detective. He often gave Frank and Joe advice on their cases.

Mr. Hardy listened to all the details Frank and Joe were telling him. "This sounds like an interesting case, boys," he said. "Look for someone who had the motive and the opportunity to take the book. Who would want the book? And who was near the book?"

Frank and Joe had a lot to think about as they fell asleep.

The next morning Frank and Joe met Chet and Iola on their usual corner. The four friends walked to school.

"I think I'll start investigating by going to the library," Frank told the others as they walked.

When they reached school, Frank walked to the library. He tried to push open the swinging door, but it was locked.

Frank looked up and down the hall. He saw Wendy Kay enter the school building through the side door.

"Wendy!" Frank called. "Hi."

Wendy turned to face Frank. "Hi, Frank," she said. Frank thought she sounded nervous. "Uh, where's Joe?" she asked.

"On the playground," Frank said. "Have you seen Ms. Goldberg?"

"Here I am, Frank," a voice called from down the hall.

Frank could see that Ms. Goldberg was carrying a lot of books. He put his backpack down outside the library door. "I can carry some of those for you," he said.

"Thank you so much, Frank." Ms. Goldberg reached in her jacket pocket for the key to the library door.

Frank looked down the hallway to see if Wendy was going to come inside the library. Wendy was gone. She probably went to find Joe, he thought.

"Ms. Goldberg," Frank began, "about *Novick's Big Book of Baseball Statis-*

tics? Do you think that you could have taken it home by mistake?"

"My goodness, no, Frank," Ms. Goldberg said. "If I had, I would have known it. That book is large. And it's heavy."

"Too bad," Frank said. "I was hoping the book would just show up today."

"Maybe it will," Ms. Goldberg said.

She opened the door. She switched on the lights as the door closed behind them.

"Do you always lock the library when you're not here?" Frank asked.

"Only at the end of the day. During the day, there's almost always somebody in here. Plus, all the books have security tags on them. An alarm goes off if somebody tries to take a book without checking it out first."

"What about *Novick's Big Book?*"

"Good thinking, Frank," Ms. Goldberg said with a smile. "I didn't tag that book. But I did keep it near me all day."

Frank left the library. He got his backpack from the hallway and went out to the schoolyard. He found Joe and their friends right where he had left them.

Just then Zack came onto the playground. He headed straight for the group of friends.

"Well, if it isn't the Hardy boys," Zack said. "Or should I say, Hardy *thieves*."

Frank shifted his backpack from one shoulder to the other.

"Take that back!" Joe said.

"Or what?" Dribbles said as he came to join Zack. "Or you two little babies are going to cry?"

Zack started to laugh. Then he grabbed Frank by the shoulders.

"Hey," Frank said. He tried to pull away from Zack. As he slipped back, Frank's backpack flew off his shoulder. It slid down his arm. As Frank went to pull it back up, Zack grabbed it in his hand. The two boys began to tug back and forth on Frank's bookbag.

"Let go!" Frank yelled.

Just then the backpack's zipper broke. A large book with a green cover fell to the ground.

"Well, what do we have here?" Zack said in a loud voice.

Everyone looked down at the book on the ground.

"Novick's Big Book of Baseball Statistics," Zack said. "What a surprise!"

Frank just stared at the book on the ground.

"Frank Hardy is the book thief!" Zack shouted.

4

Unfair!

I knew it all along!" Zack said. He pointed at *Novick's Big Book of Baseball Statistics*. "Hey, everyone!" he shouted. "I found the missing book!" Then he pointed to Frank. "Frank Hardy is a thief!"

A small crowd gathered around the boys. Everyone stared at Frank.

"What's going on?" Wendy Kay asked. She pushed her way through the crowd and stood next to Joe.

"They were fighting, then . . ." Joe

29

started to say. Then he began to cough. Then he sneezed.

Dribbles sneezed, too.

At that moment the school bell rang. But no one made a move to go into the school building. Everyone just kept staring at Frank.

"I did not steal that book!" Frank said. "I didn't."

"I believe you," Joe said.

Zack laughed. "Then how do you explain—" he started to say.

"Then how do you explain why not one of you children is in class?" a voice interrupted Zack.

Everyone recognized the voice. It belonged to the principal, Ms. Vaughn. They all turned to see her standing behind them. Then they turned their eyes back to Frank and the stolen library book. The book was still on the ground.

Ms. Vaughn walked to the middle of the circle.

"Are you two boys fighting again?" she asked Zack and Frank.

"Uh, well, ma'am," Frank said. He couldn't think of what to say. He knew it was wrong to fight. He also knew he didn't want to tattle on Zack for starting the fight. He also wondered how the stolen library book had gotten into his backpack.

"Um," Zack said, "we were just waiting here to see how Frank would worm his way out of this stolen book being found in his bag." Zack pointed to the book.

"It must have gotten there by mistake," Joe said. Then he sneezed. Wendy handed Joe a tissue.

"Thanks," Joe said.

"You're welcome," Wendy said with a smile.

Ms. Vaughn picked up the book from the ground. "This is the missing book. Do you boys know anything about it?"

"Yes," Frank said. "I mean, no."

"Well, which is it?" Ms. Vaughn asked.

"Yes, we saw the book," Joe said. "Yesterday in the library."

"But I didn't take it," Frank said. "I would never steal anything."

"Then how did it get into your backpack?" Zack asked.

"Maybe you put it there, Zack," Chet said. He stood next to Frank and Joe.

"Okay, everyone," Ms. Vaughn said. She looked at Frank. "Do you have an explanation for this?" she asked.

"No, Ms. Vaughn," Frank said.

"I am very disappointed in you, Frank," the principal said.

"But—" Frank said.

"Taking anything that is not yours is a very serious thing to do," Ms. Vaughn continued. "I'm afraid that you are going to have to stay after school for detention."

"Detention!" Joe said. "That's not fair."

"It's very good of you to stick up for your brother," Ms. Vaughn said. "But the punishment needs to fit the crime. Frank, you are going to have to work in the library after school for the next two weeks."

"But I'll miss basketball practice!" Frank said. "And that means I'll miss the big game!"

"I'm sorry, but I can't make exceptions just for sports events," Ms. Vaughn said. Then she looked at her watch.

"Okay, everyone," she said, "let's all get to our classrooms. Your teachers will be wondering where you are."

At lunchtime Chet, Frank, and Joe sat at the same table.

"Boy, that really stunk!" Chet Morton exclaimed. He took a bite of his burrito.

"So, get something else to eat," Joe said.

"I'm not talking about the food," Chet

said. "I'm talking about Frank getting punished."

"You're right about that," Joe said.

"I'd sure like to know how that book got in my backpack," Frank said. "I've been trying to figure it out all morning."

"Could you have picked it up yesterday in the library?" Joe asked. "You know, with your other books?"

"Nope," Frank said. "I emptied my backpack last night and put everything back in it this morning."

"So, that means that somebody put it there," Chet said. He took a drink of milk. "But who?"

"That's the big question," Joe said. He stirred the soup in his bowl so quickly that it almost splashed over the sides.

"Somebody set me up," Frank said. "That's what happened. I was framed."

"Sure looks that way," Chet said, "but how?"

Joe slurped a spoonful of soup. "And

when? You never let that backpack out of your sight."

"Wait," Frank said. He snapped his fingers. "I did let it out of my sight—for one second this morning. I put it down in the hallway outside of the library so I could help Ms. Goldberg. The bag seemed heavier when I picked it up."

"And that's when someone put the book in the bag!" Chet said. "So who did it?"

"Zack, of course," Joe said.

"I wish," Frank said. "But I didn't see him in the hall this morning. Somebody else must have done it."

"Who, then?" Joe said.

"Whoever was in the hall at the time," Chet answered. "So who did you see?"

"Ms. Goldberg and me," Frank started to say. "And wait—Wendy Kay!"

"Why would she take the book?" Joe asked. "And why would she take it and put it in Frank's pack?"

"Maybe she likes baseball," Chet said.

"Yeah, but why would she want to get Frank into trouble?" Joe said.

"And, anyway," Chet said, "Frank may not have seen the person in the hall before it happened. He did go into the library to help Ms. Goldberg and leave his backpack in the hall."

Frank took a piece of paper and a pencil out of his backpack. "We'll put Wendy on our suspect list anyway," Frank said. "She did have the opportunity, as Dad says."

"Who else do we put on the list?" Chet asked.

"We should add Dribbles," Joe said.

"Why?" Frank asked.

"Because wherever Zack is, Dribbles isn't far behind."

"So, Zack, Wendy, and Dribbles are our suspects," Chet said. "Looks like one of them is the thief."

5

On Zack's Trail

The three friends stared at the suspect list. Chet polished an apple and took a big bite. Joe stirred his soup with his spoon.

"If you stir that any more," Frank told his brother, "you're going to make a tornado in there."

Just as Joe stopped stirring, a wadded paper ball landed in his bowl. Soup splashed all over his shirt.

"Hey!" Joe shouted. He picked up his napkin and used it to wipe the soup off his shirt.

Chet and Frank looked around. They were hoping to see who had thrown the paper ball at Joe. They didn't see any obvious suspects.

Joe picked the paper ball out of his soup. It had floated on the surface, so it wasn't too wet.

"Hmm," Joe said. He looked at the trash can next to the lunch table. "Maybe somebody was trying to take a shot at the basket and they just missed."

Joe held the paper ball above his soup, letting drops of liquid fall back into the bowl. "If they did, though," he said, "they should apologize."

Joe turned to the trash can. He held up the paper ball as if it were a tiny basketball. He aimed and got ready to take a shot at the basket.

"Wait!" Frank said. "Let me see that paper."

"Why, do you want to lick the soup off?" Chet asked with a laugh.

"No," Frank said. "I think there's something written on it."

Joe handed the paper across the table to his brother. Frank took it by the corner. He didn't want to smudge the writing he could see on the paper.

Frank put the paper on the lunch table. He used his fingers to smooth out the paper.

Chet leaned over Frank's shoulder to look at the paper. His eyes widened. "Wow," he said. "There is definitely something written here."

"What does it say?" Joe asked.

"I think it was for Joe," Chet said. He looked at Joe and made a kissing noise with his lips.

"What?" Joe asked.

Frank turned the paper around so that his younger brother could read it.

" 'There is a girl in this school who likes you,' " Joe read aloud. "Somebody likes me? No, this must have been for Frank!"

"Not for me," Frank said. "It landed in *your* soup."

"So, I wonder who Joe's secret admirer is," Chet said.

"I don't have a secret admirer!" Joe yelled. His voice was so loud that kids at other tables looked up at him.

Joe leaned across the table. He whispered in an angry voice, "I don't have any secret admirer."

Frank looked in the direction that the paper ball had come from. He saw three different tables. All three tables had girls sitting at them.

Some of the tables had girls he knew. At one table sat Iola and her friends from second grade. Tanya Wilkins, Wendy Kay, and some other girls were at another table. And at the third table were girls he didn't recognize.

"Great," Chet said, "just what we need. A second mystery."

"Chet's right," Joe said. "Let's handle

one case at a time. We need to figure out who put that book in Frank's backpack."

"So, where do we start?" Chet asked.

"I'll bet if Zack did it, he'll eventually want to blab to somebody," Joe said. "He loves to brag."

"We'll keep an eye on him," Frank said. "Then we question whoever he talks to."

"Who's going to watch him?" Chet asked. "I have to go to the dentist this afternoon."

"It'll have to be me," Joe said. "I can follow him around after school."

"I can use my time working in the library to look around," Frank said. "I can try to figure out how the thief might have gotten the book out of the library."

"Now you sound just like Dad," Joe said.

"We *are* just like Dad," Frank said. "The best detectives in the business!"

Right after school ended for the day, Joe raced to Frank's classroom. He waited in the hallway as the kids filed out the door.

"You all set?" Frank asked.

"Yup," Joe answered.

"I'll see you later, then," Frank said. "Meet me in the library. Mom's picking us up after detention. Ms. Vaughn's already called her."

Frank headed down the hallway toward the library. Joe waited just outside the classroom door.

Soon Joe noticed Zack and Dribbles leaving the classroom.

Joe was careful to stay several yards behind Zack and Dribbles. He tried to blend into the crowd so the two boys would not know that he was following them.

Zack and Dribbles left the school building by the front door. They both walked down the steps. Then they stopped.

Joe stood inside the doorway to the school. He watched the two boys talk.

After a minute Joe could see Dribbles give Zack a high five. Then Dribbles walked away.

Zack stood on the steps alone. He looked all around him. Joe wondered if Zack was making sure he hadn't been followed. Joe pressed himself flat against the wall inside the door to make sure.

After a moment Zack turned and headed around the side of the school building. Joe rushed outside and darted down the steps. He stayed close to the building as he rounded the corner.

Zack looked over his shoulder. Again Joe pressed himself flat against the building. He wasn't sure if Zack had seen him.

Zack continued to walk. He came to a side door. That's the door near the library, Joe thought. Zack opened the door and went inside the school.

Joe ran to the side door. He crouched low to the ground and strained his neck up high enough so he could peek through the small glass window in the door.

Joe could see Zack. Zack was standing right outside the door to the library. He was talking to somebody. But Joe couldn't see who it was. The person wasn't very tall. Zack's body was blocking the person he was talking to.

Zack and the mystery person talked outside the library door for a few minutes. Joe pressed his ear against the outside door. He couldn't hear what was being said, though.

Joe went back to watching. He hoped that Zack would move. Then Joe would see who the bully was speaking to.

After another minute Joe saw the library door open.

Too bad, Joe thought. Whoever Zack was talking to has gone inside the library.

Then Joe realized that he was in big trouble. Zack turned toward the outside door. Now he could see Joe spying on him.

Zack gave Joe an angry stare. Joe stood up and backed away from the door. Zack came running at the door. He threw his full weight against it. The door swung open, barely missing Joe. Zack burst through the door. He stood in front of Joe.

"What do you think you're doing, you twerp?" Zack yelled.

6

Zack's Secret

The school door slammed closed behind Zack.

"I asked you what you're up to," Zack said again.

"I'm going to the library to see my brother," Joe said quickly.

Suddenly, the door behind Zack opened. Zack was standing too close to the building. The door bumped him from behind. Zack was thrown off balance.

"Oh, I am so sorry," a voice said from behind Zack.

Two teachers walked through the door. One reached out to put a hand on Zack's shoulder.

"Young man," the teacher said, "you really shouldn't stand so close to the door."

While Zack apologized to the teacher, Joe ran past him and into the building. He breathed a big sigh of relief and hurried into the library. He said hello to Ms. Goldberg, who was sitting at the reference table.

"Can I speak to my brother?" Joe asked the librarian.

"Well, he *is* working off his detention," Ms. Goldberg replied.

"You don't think Frank took the book, do you?" Joe asked. He really liked Ms. Goldberg. It made him sad to think she might not trust him or his brother.

"Of course not, Joe," Ms. Goldberg said. "I just can't imagine you or Frank ever doing anything like that."

Joe smiled.

"But Ms. Vaughn handed out the punishment," the librarian said. "Until we find out who really put the book in Frank's backpack, I'm afraid he has to work in the library."

"That's why I need to talk to him," Joe said. "Frank and I are working on solving the case."

Ms. Goldberg smiled. "Well, since you're here on official business, I think it would be okay for you to talk to your brother for just a few minutes."

She glanced toward the back of the library. "Frank is shelving books in the fiction section," Ms. Goldberg said. "If you give him a hand, he can leave detention early today."

"Thanks, Ms. Goldberg," Joe said.

Joe found Frank among the fiction shelves. He picked up a stack of books from a cart and began to put them in alphabetical order by each author's last name.

"Thanks for the help, little brother," Frank said. "How did it go with Zack?"

"I followed him here," Joe said. He handed his brother three books. "Could you put these on the top shelf?" he asked.

Frank took the books and put them with the *A*'s. "He came to the library?" Frank asked.

"Not inside the library," Joe answered. "But he did talk to somebody outside the library door."

"Who?" Frank asked.

"I couldn't see who it was," Joe replied. "Zack was standing in the way."

"When was this?" Frank asked. He wheeled the cart of books down the aisle to another set of shelves.

"Between five and seven minutes ago," Joe said. "I was going to follow whoever it was, but Zack saw me and came after me. And whoever he was talking to came into the library." Joe glanced around. "The person is probably still here."

"Ms. Goldberg was teaching me about shelving books," Frank said. "I was working up front until a few minutes ago. The only person who came into the library was Michael Stacy."

"I don't know who that is," Joe said.

"He's in my class," Frank answered. "He's really quiet. He's nice and very smart, too."

"He can't be too smart if he was talking to that bully," Joe said. "Maybe Zack was trying to boss him around about something."

"Let's go find out," Frank said.

Frank and Joe quickly finished putting all the books back on the shelves. Then they found Michael Stacy sitting at a table at the front of the library.

"Can we talk to you for a second?" Frank asked.

Michael looked up from the book he was reading. "Sure," he said.

"We were wondering," Frank said.

"Were you talking to Zack Jackson a little while ago?"

Michael stared at Frank for a second. Then he nodded his head.

"Did he say anything to you?" Joe asked. "About the stolen library book?"

Michael shook his head no.

"Was he bullying you?" Frank asked.

Again Michael shook his head no.

"So why were you with Zack?" Joe asked.

"I, uh, I'm not supposed to say," Michael said. "It's sort of private."

"Yeah, well, Zack is saying that Frank stole that book," Joe said. "You have to help us."

"It's really important," Frank said. "Did Zack tell you he planted the book in my backpack before school?"

"Uh, no," Michael said. "He couldn't have put it there before school."

"Why not?" Joe asked.

"Because he was with me," Michael said.

"What?" Joe asked.

"What was he doing with you?" Frank asked.

Michael looked down at his book. Then he looked up at Frank and at Joe. "Promise you won't tell?" he asked quietly.

"We promise," Frank said.

"Tell us, already," Joe said. He was beginning to feel impatient.

"Well," Michael began, "I tutor Zack in math. This morning we were going over today's homework problems. We do it almost every morning. Mrs. Burton lets us go into the classroom early."

"Wow, I never knew," Joe said.

"But you can't tell anyone," Michael said. "Zack would *kill* me if he found out."

"Your secret is safe with us," Frank told Michael.

"And so is Zack's secret," Joe said. Even though Zack was a bully, Joe didn't want to make fun of Zack for needing help with his schoolwork.

The two brothers said goodbye to Ms. Goldberg. Then they went out the back door of the school.

"Zack sure has an airtight alibi," Joe said.

"Yup," Frank answered. "We might as well move on to the next suspect."

"Okay," Joe said. "Take your choice. We have Dribbles or—"

"Look out!" Frank interrupted his brother.

Someone had thrown a basketball, and it was flying right at Joe's head!

7

Dribbles's Airtight Alibi

Frank ducked to the left. Joe ducked to the right. The basketball bounced against the wall right between the two boys. Frank caught it on the rebound.

Joe and Frank looked up to see Peter Libretti standing ten feet away.

"Dribbles!" Frank called. "The basket is over *there*." He threw the basketball back to Dribbles.

"Sorry," Dribbles said. He began to spin the ball on his index finger. Then he sneezed.

"Too much dust around here," he said.

Joe knew that Dribbles was allergic to a lot of things.

"Guess I'll have plenty of room on the court to strut my stuff," Dribbles said. "What with you having to miss the next two weeks of basketball, Frank."

"Don't be too sure, Libretti," Joe said. "My brother didn't steal that book."

"Sure, sure," Dribbles said. "The great detective team." Dribbles turned and began to walk away. "See you on the sports page, losers," he said over his shoulder.

"And that is what makes him our new number one suspect," Frank said.

"Why?" Joe asked.

"With me on detention, he gets more playing time in each game," Joe said.

"He certainly has the motive. That's what Dad says." Joe snapped his fingers. "He had the motive to want to get you in trouble."

"Now we have to prove the other

thing Dad taught us," Frank added. "We have to prove that he had the opportunity to plant the book in my bag."

"Well, you said the only time somebody could have done that was when you left the bag in front of the library this morning."

"That's right," Frank said. "Dribbles did show up late on the playground."

"Right," Joe said. "Now we have to find some clues as to where he was."

"So, let's see if Dribbles left any."

"Let's follow him home," Joe said. "See if we can dig something up."

The Hardys waited until Dribbles was done playing and left the schoolyard. Then they began to follow him. They stayed as far back as they could. They didn't want Dribbles to know he was being followed.

Dribbles came to a corner. He turned left.

"Dribbles lives in the opposite direction," Frank said. "I wonder where he's going."

"Maybe he's going over to Zack's house," Joe said. "Zack lives down that way."

Frank and Joe watched Dribbles walk almost the whole block. Joe took a step. Then he started coughing and sneezing. Joe covered his mouth, trying to muffle the noise.

"Tissue?" A voice came from behind Joe.

Joe turned around to see who was there. It was Wendy Kay. The brothers were concentrating so hard on following Dribbles that they didn't realize somebody was following them.

"What are you doing here?" Joe said. He sneezed again.

"I saw you leaving the school," Wendy said. "I thought maybe we could walk home together."

"Well, I'm sort of—Ah-choo."

60

"Gosh," Wendy said. "You still have that cold."

"I do not have a cold," Joe replied.

"Shh," Frank said. "We don't want Dribbles to know we're following him."

"Too late, Hardy boys!" Joe felt a rough hand grab him by the shoulder.

8

A Sneeze to the Rescue

Joe pushed the hand off his shoulder. He spun around.

"Dribbles!" Joe said. "What's up?"

"You know what's up," Dribbles said. "Why are you two following me?"

"We're not following you," Frank said. "We were walking Wendy home." Frank pointed to Wendy. When he turned around, he saw that Wendy was already halfway down the block. She was heading in the direction of school.

"I'll go get help," Wendy called over

her shoulder. "I won't let Dribbles beat you up!"

"Beat us—Ah-choo!" Joe sneezed.

"You, too?" Dribbles said. Suddenly he looked less angry. Then he sneezed.

"Maybe we do have colds," Joe said.

"I doubt it," Dribbles replied. "We're probably allergic to something."

"I wonder what," Joe said.

"My guess is we're allergic to Wendy's perfume," Dribbles said.

Dribbles and Joe both sniffed the air. They sneezed at the same time. All three boys began to laugh.

"Yeah," Dribbles said. "I'm allergic to a lot of things. I go to the doctor every Tuesday morning for a shot. It helps me with my allergies."

"Tuesday?" Joe said. "You mean this morning?"

"Yeah, before school," Dribbles answered. "I was almost late today."

"Then you couldn't have put the book in my backpack," Frank said.

"No," Dribbles said. "Are you still saying you were framed?"

"Of course I was framed," Frank said. "But not by you."

"Nah, I didn't do it," Dribbles said. "We may be rivals on the basketball court, but I wouldn't steal something just to get you in trouble."

"Well, thanks for being honest," Frank said. He turned to Joe. "We need to go meet Mom."

Frank and Joe said goodbye to Dribbles. They then walked back to school, where they met Mrs. Hardy.

"Hi, Mom," Joe said as he climbed into the backseat. Frank climbed in after him.

"Hi, boys," Mrs. Hardy said. "What happened to your backpack?" she asked Frank, pointing at the tear in his bookbag.

"It's a long story," Frank said.

"Start from the beginning," Mrs. Hardy told him.

On the ride home, Frank and Joe told their mother everything that had happened that day.

Later that evening Joe sat with Frank at the kitchen table. It was after dinner, and the two boys were doing their homework. Mrs. Hardy sat in the living room, sewing Frank's torn backpack.

"We got rid of two suspects today," Frank said. "We only have Wendy left."

"Don't worry," Joe said. He put his hand on his brother's shoulder. "We'll find the culprit."

"Frank," Mrs. Hardy called from the living room. "Your backpack is fixed."

"I'll get it for you," Joe said. He got up from the table and went into the living room. Joe took the backpack from his mother. He immediately began to sneeze.

"Are you coming down with a cold, Joe?" Mrs. Hardy said.

"No," Joe said. "But I think I'm coming up with a suspect."

Joe put his face close to the backpack. Then he sneezed again. "Frank, get in here!" he called.

"I'm coming!" Frank called. He ran into the living room.

"Sniff this," Joe said to Frank. He held the backpack to his brother's face.

"That smells familiar," Frank said.

Then Joe held the backpack to his own face. He inhaled, then immediately started to sneeze.

"Wendy!" The two brothers said in unison.

The next morning Frank and Joe got to the playground early. They were eager to talk to the person who had put the book in Frank's backpack.

"What's up?" Chet asked when he arrived. "I missed you guys on the walk this morning."

"We had our mom drive us," Frank

said. "We wanted to make sure we caught our thief."

"You know who it is?" Chet asked. "So, who framed Frank?"

"Wendy Kay," Joe said. He held Frank's backpack.

As Wendy approached, Joe sniffed the backpack. He sneezed. Then he stood close to Wendy. He sneezed again.

"Why did you do it?" Frank asked.

Wendy just stared at the ground.

"Why did you steal the book and put it in my backpack?" Frank asked.

"I—I," Wendy began. Then she stopped. "I didn't mean to do it! I just wanted to borrow the book overnight so I could learn about baseball. I thought that maybe Joe would like me if I knew about baseball."

"So, you're my secret admirer," Joe said.

"But why did you put the book in my backpack?" Frank asked.

"I didn't know whose backpack it

was," Wendy said. "Yesterday morning I was going to sneak into the library and put the book back. But then I saw you in the hallway. So I sneaked out again. But I saw Ms. Goldberg in there. I got nervous. The backpack was in the hall. I put the book in there. I didn't know it was yours. I'm really sorry."

"That's okay," Frank said. "But you have to tell Ms. Vaughn what you did."

"Yeah," Joe said. "You have to get my brother off the hook."

"I will," Wendy said. "Right now."

"I'll go with you," Joe said.

"Me, too," Frank added.

Joe, Frank, and Wendy walked down the hall toward Ms. Vaughn's office. "How did you know it was me?" Wendy asked.

"Your perfume," Joe said. "That's what's been making me sneeze."

"So, you don't have a cold," Wendy said. She laughed. "I'm sorry, Joe. The perfume is called Love Is in the Air. It's my older sister's. She's in high school. She wears it when she goes on a date with a boy. I guess I put on a little too much," she added.

"I guess you did," Joe said.

"I have a question for you," Frank said. "When did you get the book out of the library?"

"Remember when the lights went out on Monday?" Wendy said. Frank and Joe both nodded.

"I was standing by Ms. Goldberg's desk. You had just finished looking at the book. When the light went off, I grabbed the book. I just carried it out with my other books."

"You sure got me into a lot of trouble," Frank said. "I wish you had just found a different book on baseball to check out."

Ms. Vaughn's secretary let Frank, Joe, Chet, and Wendy go into Ms. Vaughn's office right away.

Wendy explained the whole story. "I'm sorry I took the book," she said. "And I'm sorry I got someone else in trouble," she added.

"What you did was wrong," Ms. Vaughn began. "But I admire your honesty. You will need to finish Frank's detention. And I would like you to find a way to make it up to Frank."

Just then Joe sneezed.

"There is one way you can make it up to me," Frank said. He looked at Joe.

"I know what you're going to say," Wendy said. "I promise I won't wear Love Is in the Air anymore."

"And one more thing," Joe said as the group walked back to their classrooms.

"What?" Wendy asked.

"Could you wait until high school to have a crush on me?"

"It's a deal," Wendy said. "Besides," she added, "I couldn't have a crush on someone who knows less about baseball than I do."

Everyone laughed. "Case closed," Frank said.

"Make that two cases," Joe said as he, Frank, Chet, and Wendy gave one another high fives.

BRAND-NEW SERIES!
Meet up with suspense and mystery in

#1 The Gross Ghost Mystery
Frank and Joe are making friends and meeting monsters!

#2 The Karate Clue
Somebody's kicking up a major mess!

#3 First Day, Worst Day
Everybody's mad at Joe! Is he a tattletale?

#4 Jump Shot Detectives
He shoots! He scores! He steals!

#5 Dinosaur Disaster
It's big, it's bad, it's a Bayport-asaurus! Sort-of.

By Franklin W. Dixon
Look for a brand-new story every other month
at your local bookseller

 A MINSTREL® BOOK

Published by Pocket Books

1398-04

TAKE A RIDE
WITH THE KIDS ON BUS FIVE!

Natalie Adams and James Penny have just started third grade. They like their teacher, and they like Maple Street School. The only trouble is, they have to ride bad old Bus Five to get there!

#1 THE BAD NEWS BULLY
Can Natalie and James stop the bully on Bus Five?

#2 WILD MAN AT THE WHEEL
When Mr. Balter calls in sick,
the kids get some strange new drivers.

#3 FINDERS KEEPERS
The kids on Bus Five keep losing things.
Is there a thief on board?

#4 I SURVIVED ON BUS FIVE
Bad luck turns into big fun
when Bus Five breaks down in a rainstorm.

BY MARCIA LEONARD
ILLUSTRATED BY JULIE DURRELL

A MINSTREL BOOK

Published by Pocket Books

1237-04